I Wish I Were A Butterfly

By James Howe

Illustrated by
Ed Young

VOYAGER BOOKS
HARCOURT BRACE & COMPANY
San Diego   New York   London
Printed in Hong Kong

Every story has a beginning.

This story began with a group of children at the Old Trail School in Bath, Ohio, in the fall of 1985. With sparkling eyes and waving hands and giggles of delight, they invented the tale of a cricket who thought he was ugly and a toad who made him feel that way. The story was brief, and we moved on to other things.

But I took the idea away with me and coaxed from it a middle and an end. This book is dedicated to those kindergarten, first-, and second-graders, who are older now and may not remember. I share with them the excitement of what can come of a brief moment of invention. And I thank them for what is often the hardest part of telling any story—the beginning.

—J. H.

To the late Elizabeth Armstrong, who persuaded me to play a part beyond my first book

—E. Y.

For most of the crickets in Swampswallow Pond, sunrise was a happy time. They came out of their tunnel-dark homes and celebrated the light of day with a fiddler's song.

But the littlest cricket was sad. "I want to stay here," he told his mother.

"In the dark?" she asked. "What will you do in the dark? You must come outside to make music."

"Then I won't make music," said the littlest cricket defiantly. "I don't have anything to sing about anyway."

"You don't want to come outside. You don't want to make music. The next thing you know," his mother scolded, "you *won't* want to be a cricket."

The littlest cricket sighed. Had his mother guessed his secret? "I wish I were a butterfly," he said softly. But his mother didn't hear.

"Outside with you this minute," she said.

The littlest cricket knew better
than to argue. Out into the bright
daylight he went.

But he did not make any music.

The sound of the other crickets fiddling
was more than he could bear. "Why are they
so happy being crickets?" he asked out loud.
"Perhaps they don't know what I do."

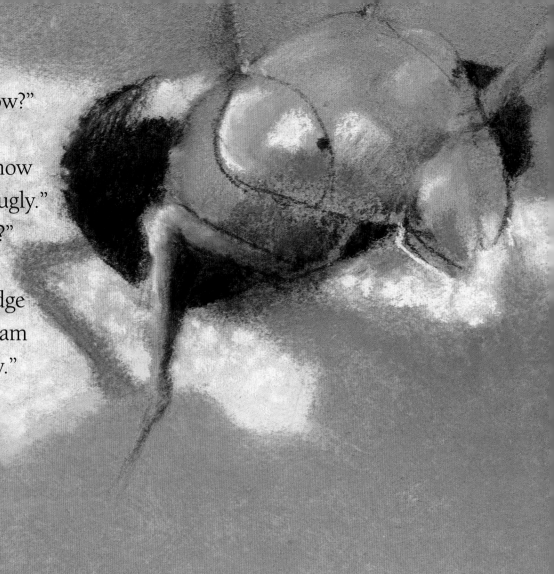

"And what is it that you know?"
asked a passing glowworm.

The littlest cricket said, "I know
that I am ugly. All crickets are ugly."

"Who told you such a thing?"
the glowworm asked.

"The frog who lives at the edge
of the pond. He told me that I am
the ugliest creature he ever saw."

"Well," said the glowworm, inspecting the littlest cricket with care, "you are not the handsomest thing in the world, but you are far from the ugliest. Look at me, I'm no beauty myself."

"But you will change into a lightning bug," the littlest cricket said, "while I will always be a cricket. An ugly, ugly cricket. I wish I were a butterfly."

"There's no use wishing for what can't be," said the glowworm, going on his way. "Being a cricket seems fine enough to me."

"That's easy for him to say," said the littlest cricket. "He will be a lightning bug one day. And the frog who lives at the edge of the pond will never find *him* ugly."

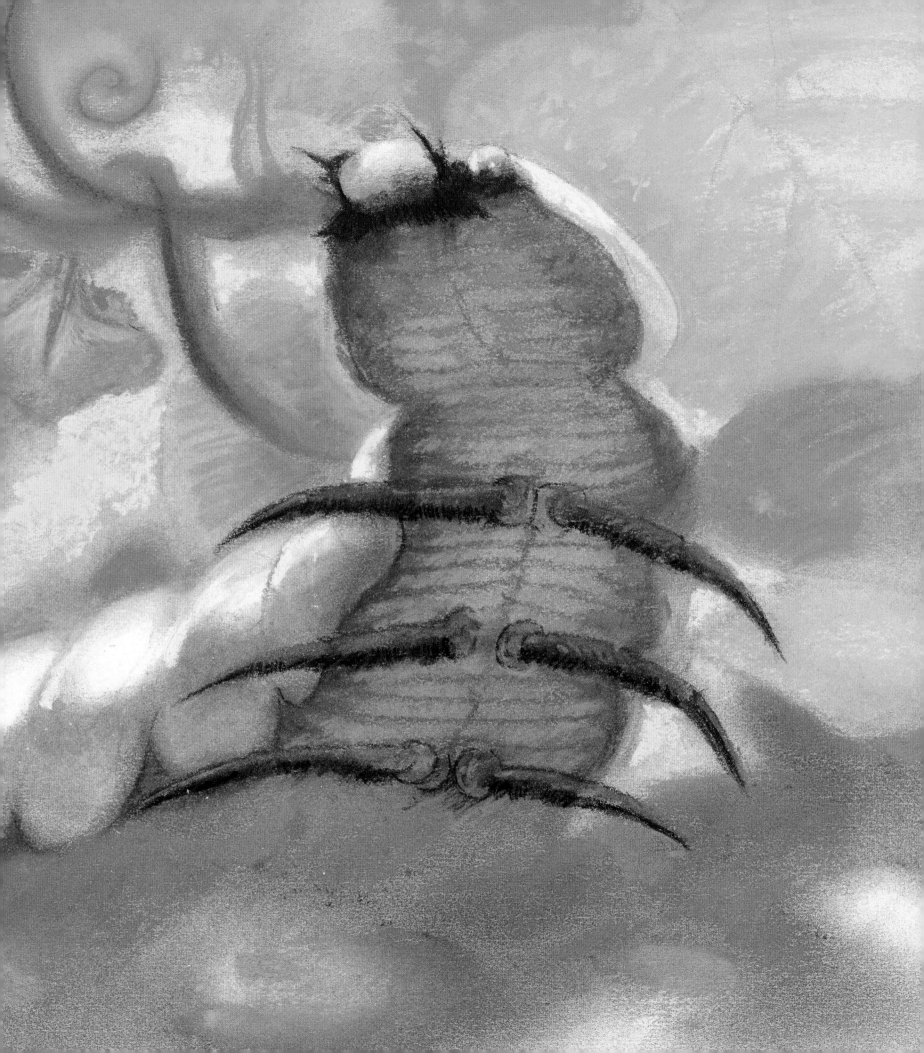

"What do you care what the frog who lives
at the edge of the pond has to say?" a
ladybug asked from atop a daisy. "If he told me
I was ugly, I wouldn't care one bit."

"But who would ever say *you* are ugly?" asked the
littlest cricket. "Everyone can see how lovely
you are. I am the color of a lump of dirt,
but you . . . you are the color of laughter,
if such a thing could be."

This amused the ladybug. "Perhaps you are right,"
she said. "But then you must learn to be
content with what you are and not mind
what a silly old frog tells you."

"That is easy for *you* to say," said the littlest
cricket as the ladybug flew away.
"Oh, I wish I were a butterfly."

He jumped onto a lily pad and drifted across the pond.

I'll talk to the Old One, he thought. She'll help me.

But seeing his reflection in the water, the littlest cricket started to cry.

"Why am I so ugly?" he asked his mirrored self. "Why can't I be—?"

"A dragonfly like me?"

The cricket looked up to see a dragonfly darting about overhead. "I couldn't help but hear your moaning and groaning," said the dragonfly. "It isn't right to be envious of others, you know. It's true that I am a magnificent creature, but so are you in your own way, I am sure."

"Hmph," said the littlest cricket. "You fly around with your whispery wings and your body all covered with jewels and tell me that *I* am magnificent? Please, Mister Dragonfly, go away. You don't understand. You can't understand. I wish I were a butterfly."

"Well, you're not a butterfly and never shall be," the dragonfly said firmly. "And wishing is a waste of time."

The littlest cricket blinked, and the dragonfly was gone. It's easy to be happy, he thought, when you are a glistening dragonfly. It's easy to be happy if you are *anything* but an ugly cricket like me.

In the middle of her web on
the other side of Swampswallow
Pond, the Old One was waiting. "I am good
at waiting," she had told the cricket once. "That is
a spider's life—spinning and waiting, waiting and spinning."

Today, when the Old One saw the littlest cricket
hop off the lily pad, she could see how sad he was. "It's a lovely day,"
the Old One called out. "And lovely days are too short to wear long faces.
What's wrong, my friend?"

"I am ugly," said the littlest cricket.